FOLKTALES OF THE WORLD

The Hungry clothes
and other jewish folktales

FOLKTALES OF THE WORLD

RETOLD BY *Peninnah Schram*

ILLUSTRATED BY *Gianni De Conno*

STERLING
New York

May all children in the world listen to each other's stories
and live in peace.

STERLING and the distinctive Sterling logo are registered trademarks of Sterling Publishing Co., Inc.

Text © 2008 Peninnah Schram
Illustrations © 2008 Gianni De Conno

ISBN 978-1-4027-9107-9

Library of Congress Cataloging-in-Publication Data

Schram, Peninnah.
 The hungry clothes and other Jewish folktales / retold by Peninnah Schram ; illustrated by Gianni De Conno.
  v. cm.
 Summary: A collection of classic Jewish folktales which emphasize values and moral lessons,
each with an introduction that places it in context with other Jewish teachings.
 Includes bibliographical references.
 Contents: Honi the circle maker — The pots of honey — The right lessons — The figs — The pomegranate seed —
The half blanket — This too shall pass — The wooden sword — The flour and the wind —
An esrog as big as a horse — Learning wisdom by observation — The wise daughter who solves riddles —
Remember — A detour through Helm — The boy who prayed with the alphabet —
A trickster teaches a lesson — The hungry clothes — Who is the laziest? — How much is a smell worth? —
King Solomon and the owl — Using your head in a tight situation — The scratched diamond.
 ISBN-13: 978-1-4027-2651-4
 ISBN-10: 1-4027-2651-1
 1. Jews—Folklore. 2. Tales. [1. Jews—Folklore. 2. Folklore.] I. De Conno, Gianni, ill. II. Title.

PZ8.1.S358Sol 2006
398.2—dc22   2007016875

For information about custom editions, special sales, and premium and corporate purchases,
please contact Sterling Special Sales at 800-805-5489 or specialsales@sterlingpublishing.com.

Manufactured in China

Lot #:
2 4 6 8 10 9 7 5 3 1

12/20

sterlingpublishing.com

Design by Lauren Rille

05213IK3/BI206/A8

contents

introduction

The stories we hear in our childhood are often the ones we remember most strongly and powerfully throughout our lives. They are usually told to us by people we know and love such as our grandparents, parents, and teachers. We associate these stories with the people who told them to us and incorporate the values, faith, traditions, and ethical lessons from those stories into our lives.

In Judaism, stories and storytelling are major tools for learning and passing along the Jewish faith, culture, and tradition. The first stories a child hears are often biblical tales about the creation of the world. These stories, along with others, instill and nourish a sense of wonder and curiosity about the world and about God. They are often read to us, but may also be told from memory. The Jewish culture has a vital oral tradition that encompasses folktales, fairy tales, legends, parables, fables, tall tales, trickster and fool tales, supernatural tales, and mystical tales. Some of these tales come from the Talmud, which is a collection of commentaries on the Torah.

Others are found in medieval rabbinic collections, in various Hasidic tales, and in the Ashkenazic and Sephardic folklore. Without a doubt, most of these tales were transmitted orally before they were written down.

A great many Jewish folktales and legends portray the shared religious themes of Judaism and contain beloved characters such as King Solomon. In folktales, these biblical characters become popularly known for a specific expertise. For example, King Solomon becomes the master of wisdom. The names of rabbis may differ from story to story, and certain themes are emphasized differently because of the many locations where the Jews lived. Many folktales and legends have been "borrowed" from other cultures and therefore have more secular (not religious) themes, plots, and characters. Regardless of their origin, the common denominator of all Jewish tales is that they carry a message that resonates with Jewish values, ethics, traditions, and ideals.

In this collection of Jewish folktales, I chose to include stories that I love to tell. My goal was to find stories that use wisdom, humor, and resourceful thinking to reflect Jewish values and moral lessons. Several of these tales I heard as a child. Many I re-dicovered as I searched through the Talmudic texts and collections of Jewish folktales, while others I found more recently in the Israel Folktale Archives. In many of these stories, the main characters have to use their wisdom and wits to solve a problem, to teach someone a lesson, or to save themselves from a predicament.

In some of the stories, I made a few changes to the folktale. For example, the character of the judge in "The Pots of Honey" is usually King David or his son, Solomon. I chose to replace the king with a wise woman as the storyteller who serves as judge and advice-giver. I modeled the problem-solver after the female storytellers of Eastern Europe who were known in their communities as advice-givers. In "How Much Is a Smell Worth?" I took another folktale usually associated with King Solomon, set it in Marrakesh, and introduced the Hakham as the wise judge. I used details

that I learned from my son-in-law, who lived in the Moroccan city as a young boy, including the relationship between the king and the Jews, and the names of certain pastries. Many of the tales in this book can also be found in the folklore of other countries.

Since folktales are most effective when shared among the generations, my hope is that you will share these stories with parents and grandparents, as well as with other family members and teachers. Perhaps these stories will trigger the memory of other family, ethnic, or traditional tales. Maybe personal and family stories prompted by one of these folktales will become part of the bigger story. Adding these stories to the holiday tales could lead to creating new rituals. My hope is that telling and reading stories will become a more active ritual on the Sabbath, at holy day gatherings, at bedtime, in the classroom, and at any time when family and friends are together. In this way, the oral tradition can continue, ever new, ever renewing, and ever vital.

Now let's tell some folktales!

Honi the Circle Maker

One of the legendary Jewish heroes, Honi the Circle Maker was a miracle worker who lived in the first century CE. Through this story, we come to understand how much the Jewish tradition treasures trees. We also learn that we must take care of our earth and not deplete it of its resources. Rather, we must ensure that resources are left for future generations.

Honi the Wise One was also known as Honi the Circle Maker. In times of need, Honi would draw a circle, step inside of it, and recite special prayers for rain. Sometimes during a drought, he would even argue with God. At those times, Honi would say, "I refuse to step outside of this circle until the rain begins to fall." And the rains would come. He was, indeed, a miracle maker.

As wise as he was, Honi sometimes saw things that puzzled him. At those times, he would ask questions to help him unravel the mystery.

One day as Honi the Circle Maker was walking down the road, he saw an old man planting a carob tree. After greeting the man, Honi asked him, "How long will it take for this tree to bear fruit?"

The old man replied, "Seventy years."

Then Honi asked the old man, "And do you think you will live long enough to eat the fruit of this tree?"

The old man answered, "Perhaps not. But when I was born, I found many carob trees planted by my father and grandfather. Just as they planted trees for me, I am planting trees for my children and grandchildren so that they will be able to enjoy eating the trees' fruit. Then it will be up to them to plant more trees for future generations."

And so this has been the Jewish tradition ever since.

The pots of honey

Trusting friends is a common theme in many Jewish folktales. But what can one do to prove the truth when something happens to break that trust? That's when a creative solution is needed to achieve the most prized of all Jewish goals—justice. According to Jewish tradition, once the truth is revealed, the resolution must involve asking for and granting forgiveness—both highly valued actions in Judaism.

A long time ago, there lived a young widow named Devorah. One day she heard that her mother, who lived in a distant land, was gravely ill and needed her help.

Devorah had been saving her money since her husband had died. She had some gold that her husband had left for her and some that she had earned by selling her beautiful embroidery. She kept her gold coins hidden in pots of honey. Devorah knew that she would have to leave the heavy pots behind and take only enough money for her food and travel. But she had a problem. What was she to do with the precious pots of honey? To leave them in her home would be too much of a risk. There were always robbers traveling through the communities, and she didn't want her gold to be stolen.

Devorah had a neighbor named Yoel whom she trusted to keep her money safe until she could return home. She brought the three honey pots to Yoel and said, "My good neighbor, I don't know how long I will be away. I trust that you will keep my three pots of honey for me until my return. I know that they will be secure with you. When I return, I shall bake some special honey pastries for you." Then Devorah packed her belongings and set off on the long journey to see her mother.

Soon after Devorah left, Yoel needed some honey for his son's wedding pastries. "Why not use the honey from Devorah's pots?" he reasoned. "I can easily replace it when she returns." But when Yoel began to empty the pots of honey, he discovered the gold coins at the bottom of each pot. "Hmmm, I can make good use of these gold coins," he mused. "Who knows if or when Devorah will return. And if she does return, I'll deny that she gave me pots filled with anything but honey. After all, she would not be able to prove that she gave me any gold."

With that, Yoel emptied the pots of honey. With Devorah's gold coins, he had more than enough money not only for his son's wedding celebration, but also for fine new clothes and jewelry for his entire family. After the wedding, Yoel poured honey back into the pots, covered them, and placed them on a high shelf.

Some time later, Devorah's mother died and she returned home. Devorah immediately went to her neighbor's house. Yoel was shocked to see her, but pretended to be happy. He invited her to come inside.

"I am very glad to be home," she said. "I have come to ask for the three pots of honey that I left with you."

"Of course, my dear Devorah. They are safe on a shelf. I shall climb up to get them for you," Yoel replied with a halfhearted laugh.

When Devorah brought the pots home, she uncovered them and looked inside. But instead of gold coins, she found only honey. She immediately ran back to her neighbor.

"There must be some error. You have mistakenly given me your pots filled with honey. My pots had gold coins hidden in the honey."

"Ah, no, these are the very pots of honey that you left with me. You can see the markings on the side. These are yours, just as you left them," Yoel insisted.

What was Devorah to do? If she accepted his word, she would remain penniless. As she left her neighbor's house, she protested, "These could not be my pots. Mine were filled with the gold coins that I had saved." But by the time she had finished speaking, Yoel's door was already closed. Devorah wept bitterly.

A few days later, she decided to bring the case to

the local wise woman, Hannah, who was also the storyteller for the women of the community. In the evenings, the women would gather at Hannah's home to hear stories filled with women's wisdom. These stories warmed their hearts as they embroidered tablecloths or crocheted blankets.

Whenever a woman had a question or a problem, she would go to Hannah the Storyteller. Sometimes she would have a long wait, because other women had come before her and Hannah liked to talk to each woman alone. Listening carefully, Hannah would turn the gold ring on her finger. Then she would answer the question with a folk remedy or solve the problem with a proverb or a story. Sometimes Hannah would ask a question and wait until the woman bringing the problem suddenly stood up with a sigh and an exclamation that she now understood what she needed to do.

And so Devorah told Hannah the Storyteller about her pots of honey and that her neighbor, Yoel, had denied taking the gold coins hidden in the pots. Then she added, "It's not fair! It's not just! My neighbor is not telling the truth, but what can I do? I have no possible way to prove that he is lying."

"You know," Hannah said, "there's a saying, 'A friend is a friend until he reaches into your pocket.' Devorah, were there any witnesses when you gave your neighbor the pots of honey?"

"No, there was no one else present. I trusted his word alone. What can I do now?" wept Devorah.

Hannah began to turn her gold ring. "There's another saying, 'A thief has a good heart for he takes pity on others' possessions.' Devorah, where are those pots of honey now?" she asked.

"They are still in my neighbor's house. I brought them back to him when I discovered that the gold coins were missing. What did I want with pots of honey?"

Suddenly Hannah said, "Aha! I have an idea that is worthy of King Solomon himself. We will go and visit your neighbor right now. Come with me."

Hannah threw her shawl over her shoulders and walked with Devorah to Yoel's house. When Yoel answered the knock on the door, he was surprised to see the two women. He reluctantly invited them into his house and asked, "What brings you both here?"

"Do you have the three pots of honey that Devorah gave to you for safe-keeping?" asked Hannah the Storyteller.

"Of course I do. Here they are." And Yoel put the pots on the table.

"Good," said Hannah. "Now bring me three neighbors whom you trust." And Yoel went to get three of his neighbors.

When they were all gathered, Hannah once again turned to Devorah's neighbor. "Devorah claims that she gave you three pots filled with honey and gold coins, but you say that Devorah gave you pots filled only with honey? Is that right, Yoel?" she asked.

"That's right. I kept the pots on a high shelf and didn't touch them until she returned to claim them. They contained only honey and nothing more," Yoel replied defiantly.

"Very well then," continued Hannah the Storyteller. "We'll see about that. I want you to empty the honey from Devorah's pots into some bowls." Yoel did as she requested.

"Now," Hannah continued, "break those pots open in front of your neighbors whom you trust!"

Yoel was confused by this command. "But why?" he asked. "What will that prove?" He knew that Hannah the Storyteller was a wise woman and often solved problems for the community. People accepted her judgments without question. While he would not admit it, even Yoel was awed by her presence in his home.

Hannah did not say another word. She simply stood there waiting.

Yoel took a hammer and broke the three pots. Hannah picked up some of the large shards and looked at them carefully. Then she pointed to the inside of them. "Look," she said. "Here are two gold coins that you did not take because they were stuck to the sides of the pots. This proves that what Devorah said is the truth. She gave you pots filled with both honey and gold coins. You, her good neighbor, took her gold coins for your own use. We have a saying, 'He's not a thief. He only takes if it happens to be there in front of him.' Now, Yoel, in order to restore your good name, you must apologize and return to Devorah the full amount that you took from her."

Shamed into admitting that he had stolen Devorah's gold coins after all, Yoel gave back all of her money.

"Forgive me, Devorah. I was wrong and regret what I did. I have learned my lesson. I shall never steal from anyone again," he promised her.

Hannah the Storyteller looked at Yoel and said, "Our sages say, 'Wisdom and regret come too late.'"

But Devorah, seeing that her neighbor was truly sorry, forgave him.

the Right Lessons

In this story, we meet Rabbi Joshua, son of Hananya, a familiar historical character who also appears in Jewish folktales. Joshua was one of the great scholars who taught the Talmud orally in the first to second centuries CE, because Oral Law was not allowed to be written down. These teachers became known as "living books." Joshua's stories demonstrate the Jewish belief that we can learn from everyone—not just from great scholars or highly placed people.

Although Rabbi Joshua was not a handsome man, he WAS a great teacher and a great scholar. Joshua knew how to teach a lesson using words like arrows that reached their mark.

One day the daughter of the emperor Hadrian said to Rabbi Joshua, "What a pity! Such great wisdom in so ugly a vessel!"

Perhaps someone else would have replied with another insult, but not Joshua. Instead, he asked a question. "Your father has a huge storehouse of wines. In what kind of vessels does he keep this wine?"

"Why, in earthenware vessels, of course," the princess answered quickly.

"But ordinary people also keep their wine in earthenware vessels. You are important people. You should keep your wine in vessels of finer material such as silver or gold."

This sounded fitting, so the princess found her father and told him that the emperor's wine should be put into silver and gold vessels. Since the emperor never denied his daughter any request, and because he was too busy with important matters to realize what she was asking, the emperor ordered that it be so. But soon all the wine in the royal winery turned sour.

"Who gave you this advice, Daughter?" asked the emperor.

When Hadrian heard his daughter's reply, he summoned Rabbi Joshua to the palace and said, "My daughter tells me that you advised her to keep our royal wines in vessels of silver and gold. Why did you give my daughter this advice? It seems that wine can only stay preserved in earthenware vessels."

"Ah, indeed, that is true," Rabbi Joshua said. Then he turned to the emperor's daughter and added, "So, too, can a person who is not handsome contain great wisdom."

And so the princess learned two valuable lessons at once.

One day Rabbi Joshua was eating a meal with his friends. "Joshua, I have noticed that at every meal we eat together, you always leave a little bit of food on your plate. Why is that?" one of his friends asked.

"That is true. I always leave a mouthful or more of food on the plate. You see, I learned a good lesson from a woman I once met. It was when I was a very young man and had stopped at an inn for a few days. On the first day, the owner prepared a meal of beans for me. She placed the pot on the table and I ate every last bean. When she served me the same meal the next day, again I finished everything in the pot. On the third day, she salted the food so much that I stopped eating after I had taken the first bite.

"The woman came over to the table and asked me, 'What is wrong? I see that you are not finishing your meal.'

"'Oh, I have already eaten a big meal today. I am not very hungry after all,' I replied.

"'Ah, but you washed your hands and recited the blessing over the bread. You would not have done that if you had already eaten. No, you are leaving the food that you should have left for the servants and the poor these last two days. As the wise men say, "No food need be left in the pot for those in need, but something must be left for them on the plate."'

"When she said that, I realized that we must always remember the poor. Now I always leave some food on my plate and put some money into the charity box," Rabbi Joshua explained.

By now, his friends were curious. Another of the friends asked, "Rabbi Joshua, you are known as a great teacher. What other lessons were you taught?"

"I remember two lessons that a wise young girl taught me. Sometimes we can learn more from children if we will only listen to them," replied Rabbi Joshua.

"Once when I was on a journey, I came to a crossroads. I didn't know which way to turn. There near the side of the road was a young girl picking some flowers. I called out to her with a greeting of peace and said, 'I seem to be lost. Which road leads to the town?'

"The young girl approached the wagon and replied, 'This road is long but short, and that other road is short but long.' As she spoke, she pointed first to one road and then to the other. I continued along the second road, the one that was 'short but long.' All seemed to be going well until I arrived at some vineyards and orchards. I could see the town on the other side, but there was no road going through them. So I had to take the road back to the crossroads. When I returned, the young girl was still there. 'Why did you tell me that this road is short?' I asked.

"The young girl laughed at me and said, 'You see that you could not approach the town directly through the vineyards and orchards. Instead you had to return to this point. It's true that this road to the town is short, but it is also long because you had to travel around the vineyards to reach the town. The other road is long, but it will take you directly into the town.'

"As I was about to leave, I noticed that the girl had picked up a covered basket. 'What is in that basket?' I asked her.

"At that point, she turned to me and simply responded, 'This basket is covered, sir, so that others will not see what I do not wish them to see.'

"With that, the young girl picked up her bouquet of flowers and went in the direction of her home.

"I learned two valuable lessons from that wise young girl. Not only did I learn that I must listen carefully when I ask a question, but I also learned when I should not ask a question."

The figs

The first fruit mentioned in the Torah, the fig represents peace and symbolizes the promise and blessing of the Land of Israel. This story about a gift of figs teaches us the importance of giving with our whole hearts. In Judaism, the reward for performing a good deed (or mitzva) is the good deed itself. Doing something only to get a reward diminishes the value of both the action and the person.

One day the emperor went for a ride in the country. Along his path he met an old man who was planting a fruit tree. The emperor got off his horse and asked with great curiosity, "Tell me, old man, why are you planting a tree that will take time to bear fruit? Why not let your children work and plant?"

The old man replied, "Your Majesty, I plant trees because my father and grand-father planted trees before me. You see, when I was born, there were already many trees in the world that they had planted. Now it is my turn to plant trees for my children and grandchildren. This is a fine fig tree," he added, pointing to its bare, thin branches.

"Ah, I do like figs very much. When you gather the figs from this tree, bring them to the palace. I would like to eat some of them. May you be blessed with many more years of life so that you can continue planting trees and eating figs," the emperor said as he got back on his horse.

Soon the fig tree grew leaves and blossomed. Finally some figs appeared. When the tree was four years old, the old man gathered a basketful of figs and went to the emperor's palace. At first the guards would not allow him to enter. They thought he was a beggar or a crazy man. Why else would he be bringing a basket of figs to the great and wealthy emperor? But the old man insisted that he had come at the invitation of the emperor.

"Tell him that the old man who was planting a fig tree has come with a delicious gift—figs from the young tree," the old man instructed the guards.

The guards reappeared and brought the old man before the emperor. When the emperor tasted the figs, he was overjoyed with their fragrance and sweetness. He immediately ordered the treasurer to fill the old man's basket with gold coins. The emperor thanked the old man for his gift of figs and again blessed him with long life.

When the old man returned home with the basket of gold, his neighbor saw him. Curious to know where he had been and what was in the basket, he invited the old man for tea. As they sat and talked, he said to the old man, "I see that you are dressed in your finest clothes. No doubt you had to visit an important person." So the old man told his neighbor about meeting the emperor years before while planting the fig tree and how he had just returned from the palace.

"I brought the emperor a basketful of figs, and he was so grateful that he filled my basket with gold coins," the old man related to his neighbor.

As soon as the old man left, the neighbor's greedy wife said, "Husband, since the emperor likes figs so much, fill this basket with them. Then go directly to the palace and ask to see the emperor. Give him the figs and wait for him to fill your basket with gold coins, too." And she handed her husband her largest basket and pushed him out the door.

The neighbor quickly filled the basket with ripe figs and hurriedly went to the palace. He explained that he had a basket of figs and demanded to see the emperor. The emperor happened to be passing by and heard the neighbor shouting his demands at the guards.

"Why do you want to see me?" the emperor asked.

"My old neighbor came with a basket of figs and you rewarded him with gold coins. I, too, have brought figs for you. Does that not deserve a reward?" asked the neighbor.

"Ah, when your old neighbor brought those figs, he gave the gift with his whole heart and without expecting a reward. But here is what you deserve," replied the emperor as he led the neighbor to the gate of the palace. "Stand here and all who pass will take some figs from your basket and throw them at you."

When the basket was emptied, the neighbor returned home. His wife was at the door waiting for him. When she saw the empty basket, she demanded to know what had happened.

"Dear wife, you and your foolish ideas! Gold for figs! I only got figs for figs. However, I am thankful for one thing—that it was only soft figs people threw at me and not hard lemons!"

The pomegranate seed

Pomegranates are one of the seven species of agricultural produce that symbolize the fertility of the Land of Israel. A pomegranate is a magnificent fruit in shape and color. According to Jewish tradition, the pomegranate contains 613 juicy seeds that represent the 613 religious commandments, or mitzvot.

A long time ago, there lived a man who was so poor that his children often went to sleep hungry at night. As hard as he worked as a cobbler, the man could not earn enough to feed his family. He wept when there was not enough food in his home, especially on Shabbat.

One day the cobbler was walking near a bakery. Even though he had no extra money in his pockets, the smell of fresh bread baking drew him closer to the store. As he was lingering near the breads, the sudden thought came into his head to take a loaf. "Not only do my children need this bread, but the baker would not miss one loaf," he said under his breath. Then he promised himself, "I'll pay the baker for the loaf when I save some money."

The cobbler grabbed the loaf of bread and put it under his coat, but the baker saw him and shouted, "Thief! Thief!" The sultan's soldiers arrived immediately and arrested the poor man. The cobbler was afraid for his life. He knew that the penalty for theft was death.

What was he to do? No matter how hard life was, he had never stolen anything before. His wife would worry when he did not arrive home as usual. And the children…As the cobbler tried to think about what to do, something hit him in the face. The hooves of a horse had kicked up some dirt along with the skin and kernels of a pomegranate. The cobbler wiped his face and looked at a pomegranate kernel. Suddenly he had an idea. He began muttering to himself just loudly enough for the sultan's soldiers to hear.

"If only the sultan knew my secret, I know he would let me live. If only I could speak with the sultan and tell him my wonderful secret. When the sultan hears this secret, he will surely reward his soldiers handsomely."

When the soldiers heard this, they said to each other, "Perhaps the sultan will reward us if he likes this secret. If not, the man will die as planned." They decided to bring the cobbler directly to the sultan.

"What is this wonderful secret?" asked the sultan curiously.

"O Sultan, I have a secret that was handed down from my great grandfathers to my father and now to me. I hold in my hand a pomegranate kernel that will grow into a tree and bear fruit overnight. Each luscious pomegranate will be filled with 613 kernels."

The sultan had always been a curious man, and he wanted to see if this could truly happen. He said to the poor cobbler, "Really! That must be a magical

seed. We shall see. You must spend this night in prison. Tomorrow morning you will be brought to the royal garden and we will plant your seed. If it does not grow into a tree with pomegranates on it the next morning, you shall immediately be put to death. If a tree does grow, as you say it will, then you shall be free to return home."

The cobbler smiled slightly as he nodded to the sultan and was taken to the prison.

Early the next morning, the soldiers brought the cobbler to the royal garden. Soon the sultan arrived, surrounded by his advisors and his guards. The gardener had already dug a small hole in which to plant the pomegranate kernel.

The sultan gave a signal to begin the planting. But as the cobbler bent over to put the seed in the ground, he quickly straightened up and said, "O Sultan, the one condition that I learned from my father is that only an honest man who has never stolen or taken anything can plant this seed or else it will not grow. I just realized that I am a thief because I stole a loaf of bread for my hungry children. I can no longer have the honor of planting this seed."

Turning to the vizier, the cobbler said, "But you, the sultan's trusted chief advisor, surely you can plant this seed."

The vizier waved away the hand holding the pomegranate kernel and said in a quiet voice, "Aaaaaaah, I am not the one who can plant this seed. You see, many years ago someone gave me good advice for the sultan. I did give him that advice, but I claimed it as my own idea. I took something away from that man—the chance for his promotion in the royal court and a reward in exchange for his wise advice."

Then the cobbler turned to the royal treasurer. "You are a most reliable and worthy treasurer. The sultan entrusts his entire fortune to you. No doubt you are an honest person. Come plant this pomegranate seed so that the sultan can have fresh pomegranates on his plate tomorrow morning."

The treasurer bowed his head and whispered, "I'm afraid I cannot plant this seed. Not so long ago, I was to give a worthy person a deserved and great reward from the sultan, but I took a portion of that reward for myself and did not tell anyone about it."

"Well, O Sultan, it appears that you are without a doubt the most honest man in the country. Take the seed and plant it yourself. The pomegranates that appear for the plucking in the morning will be filled with more promise," said the cobbler as he gave the kernel to the sultan.

"I'm afraid that I cannot plant the seed either," the sultan said in a soft voice and admitted that he had taken a medal from one of his soldiers.

"O Sultan, you and your advisors are all so powerful and have achieved such high status and wealth. And yet you have not been honest and so cannot plant this pomegranate kernel. I am a poor man who only wanted to live a life without shame, yet because of my terrible poverty, I stole one loaf of bread for my family. It's true that stealing even so little is wrong, but..."

Suddenly the sultan burst out laughing. "You are a clever man, after all. You have taught us all a very important lesson. For this you shall never go hungry again. Not only will I pay the baker for that loaf of bread, but you will be pardoned as well. I shall also give you a great reward, which the treasurer will bring to you personally—and the full amount at that. Now return home with my gratitude."

Happily, the cobbler returned home in the sultan's carriage. Soon after that, the treasurer brought him a chest filled with gold and a large basket of pomegranates.

The flour and the wind

One of the most popular folklore heroes in Jewish oral tradition, King Solomon is known as the wisest man in the world. In folktales and legends, Solomon usually judges cases that call for creative decisions. Since evenhanded justice is a treasured goal in Judaism, the judge who can resolve difficult cases is certainly someone who deserves great respect.

Once there was a devout woman named Rebekah who lived in Jerusalem. Every day she baked four loaves of bread. Three of the loaves she gave to the poor beggars who came daily to her door. One loaf of bread she kept for her family meals. This is what she always did.

One day after she had given the three breads away, a fourth beggar came to Rebekah's door. What did she do? She gave that beggar her fourth loaf of bread. When Rebekah saw that she had no more flour in her barrel to bake another bread, she took some corn to the grindstone near the seashore and ground the corn into flour.

As was her custom, Rebekah put the sack of flour on her head and began the walk back to her home. Suddenly the sky became dark and a storm arose. A strong gust of wind whirled around her head and blew the sack of flour out to sea.

Rebekah ran in the direction of the sack, crying out, "What did I do to deserve this injustice! What will I feed my family now?" But the wind swallowed up her words and the rain mixed with her angry tears. Since there was no one to hear her, she turned away from the sea and began the walk home empty-handed.

On her way home, she changed directions again and went directly to the court of King Solomon. When the guards saw how determined she was, they immediately brought her to the king. She began to tell King Solomon about

the sack of flour and how it had blown out to sea, but then there was a great commotion as ten men carrying ten sacks of gold burst into the room.

"We want to give these bags of gold to the person who saved our lives," one of them said. "If we cannot find that person, we will donate the gold to the poor people in this community."

King Solomon was listening with great interest. He asked, "What do you mean 'saved your lives'?"

"We were sailing close to the harbor when our ship suddenly began to sink. There was a hole in the ship and water was coming in fast. The ship would have sunk and we would have drowned."

"That is certain," said a second man.

Then a third man continued the story. "But just as suddenly, the water stopped flooding in. When we examined the hole, we found a bag of flour there. The flour had mixed with the water and turned into dough. The dough plugged up the hole and stopped the water from flooding our ship."

"The sack of flour saved us, and now we want to reward the person whose sack it is," a fourth man added. He pulled the sack out of his pocket and handed it to King Solomon.

Taking the sack, Solomon laughed out loud and turned to the woman standing there as still as a statue. She could hardly believe what was happening. "Rebekah," he said, "would you recognize your sack? Does it have any special markings?"

"Yes. I always embroider my name on my sacks," she said.

When Solomon examined the sack, he found her embroidery. "Is this your sack?"

"Yes," replied Rebekah. "That is indeed my sack."

Then Solomon said, "It is you who deserves to receive the reward from these grateful men. Your sack of flour saved them. Without it, they surely would have drowned. Wondrous indeed are the ways of the Creator."

Then Solomon blessed the woman, and she returned home with a renewed sense of wonder and justice.

the half blanket

While this story illustrates the commandment "Honor your father and your mother," it also emphasizes the Jewish teachings of creating peace in the family. The important lessons of showing respect for your elders, being a role model for the young, and knowing how to right your mistakes are equally important to the Jewish culture.

A long time ago, there was a wealthy man who had one son. As the father grew older, the son grew up. He began to work with his father and became a successful merchant. Soon he married, and he and his wife had a child.

One day the old father said, "My son, I can no longer work in our business. I have confidence that you will continue to keep our good name as honest businessmen. I have decided to give you everything now, while I am still alive. You will have all my property and wealth. In that way, I, too, can enjoy your success. I'm sure that I will have what I need."

The son was overjoyed and thanked his father.

In the beginning, the son honored his father and gave him daily reports on the business, often asking for his advice.

As time went on, however, the son began to talk only occasionally to his father. When his father offered suggestions, the son interrupted him by saying sharply, "I know what I am doing. I don't need your help."

Then there came a day when the son said to his father, "I don't need any more of your advice. Now that I own this property, I want you to leave."

"Where shall I go? I am too old to leave my home," replied the father.

"Well, old man," answered his son, "you had better leave by sunrise, or I shall have you thrown out."

So the old father left his home. He began to wander the streets begging for food or coins.

One very cold day, the old father walked by his son's home. He saw his young grandchild playing in the yard and explained who he was.

Then he said, "Please, dear child, ask your father to give me a blanket so that I may be warm in this frost."

The child ran to his father. "Dear father, please give me a blanket for the old man who says he is your father. Is it true that he is my grandfather? Please tell me where to find a blanket for him."

"Very well," replied the young father. "Go to the attic and there you'll find an old blanket. You may take it to your grandfather."

The child ran up the stairs to find the blanket. After a while, the young father began to wonder what his son was doing up in the attic. When he reached the room, he saw his child trying to cut the blanket with a knife.

"What are you doing, my child?" he asked.

"I am cutting this blanket in half, Father, so that I can give half to my grandfather. I am going to keep the other half for you. When you grow old and go out to beg in the cold, I'll give you this part of the blanket to keep you warm," said his son.

The young father raced down the stairs and ran out the front door to where the boy's grandfather was waiting in the cold.

"Forgive me, my father, for what I have done to you. You deserve my gratitude and honor for all you have given me. I have forgotten the honor that you deserve. Please come inside and be in your home once again," pleaded the young father.

The old man forgave his son.

That night, as the grandfather was sitting in his chair near the fireplace, the grandchild came up to him and sat on his lap. The child held the two halves of the blanket. The old man took one half for his lap and covered the lap of the child with the other half. Then the old man winked and began telling a story to his grandchild. And that's how it was for many years.

this too shall pass

This story introduces King Solomon as a happy trickster who enjoys competition, especially when he is the one challenging his friend. But as Solomon learns from his trick, happiness and despair are equally fleeting. His story serves to remind us that balance and moderation are a necessary part of the Jewish way of life.

King Solomon asked many questions of his trusted friend and advisor, Benaiah, who was almost as wise and as handsome as Solomon himself. Benaiah always answered with great confidence and wisdom for he, too, was a great scholar. Benaiah was also a loyal friend. He always did whatever King Solomon asked of him without question.

One day Solomon said to Benaiah, "My friend, I am seeking an extra-ordinary ring that has the power to make a happy man sad and a sad man happy. I am sending you on a mission to find such a ring. But you must return in thirty days."

Solomon knew that such a ring did not exist, but he enjoyed having the power to send his friend on a fool's errand. Always a competitive man, Solomon tried to find ways to see if he could outwit his friend. He enjoyed playing chess with Benaiah, but just the week before he had lost a game to him. Perhaps Solomon was still feeling the sting of this loss. It had never happened before and he wanted to teach his friend a lesson.

Solomon was certain that Benaiah would return in thirty days without the ring. Then he could laugh at seeing his friend humbled. But Solomon was also looking forward to hearing about Benaiah's adventures along the way. He was sure that they would still be good friends when he explained that he had sent Benaiah on a fool's errand. Besides, discussing the trip would give them many evenings of diversion from the serious business of ruling a kingdom.

The next morning, Benaiah set out on his journey to find the special ring. Trusting his friend, he never stopped to think that Solomon might be playing a trick on him.

Benaiah rode his horse from place to place in search of the ring. He stopped at jewelers' shops and wandered into crafts stalls and marketplaces in each town he came to. Everywhere he stopped, he asked, "Do you know of a special ring that would make a happy man sad and a sad man happy?"

Whenever he asked that question, the jewelers looked at him as though he were a madman. "How can a ring make a happy man sad and a sad man happy? That is impossible. You are surely on a fool's errand," they all told him.

It was nearly the end of the thirty days when Benaiah returned to Jerusalem. For the first time, he was certain that he would fail his beloved king. He was walking along a narrow, crooked street when he passed a small shop filled with rings and thought, "I will try this one last place."

Entering the shop, he saw the jeweler and his apprentice working side by side. Benaiah waited until the jeweler looked up. Then he asked, "Do you know of a special ring that can turn a happy man into a sad man and a sad man into a happy man?" Expecting the jeweler to reply with a laugh, as they all had done up until now, Benaiah began to leave.

"Of course I know of such a ring. In fact, I have just such a ring. Wait here," answered the jeweler.

The jeweler went to the back of the shop. He returned a few moments later with a plain gold ring in his hand. When Benaiah looked closer, he was able to see three Hebrew letters engraved on the ring: gimel, zayin, yud. Benaiah laughed out loud, his spirits lifted. He thanked the jeweler and gave him a great sum of money in exchange for the ring.

Benaiah quickly rode back to Solomon's palace. Seeing Benaiah enter the throne room, Solomon began to anticipate how amused he would be when Benaiah told him that he had failed.

Instead, Benaiah strode up to the king and handed him the gold ring. King Solomon looked at it. Then he looked closer and saw the three Hebrew letters. His laugh froze on his face as he realized what they stood for: *Gam zeh ya'avor*— "This too shall pass."

After a few moments, Solomon's face grew somber and he said, "I now realize that all my great wisdom and power is only for the moment. One day another will sit on my throne."

Then, turning to his friend, Solomon said, "Benaiah, you have proven once again to be a faithful and wise friend. What's more, you have taught me a great lesson. For that, I thank you with a grateful heart."

Benaiah had succeeded in his quest for the extraordinary ring.

the wooden sword

In Judaism, a person establishes a direct relationship or dialogue with God. By reciting "Blessed be God, day by day," the young hero in this tale reaffirms both this relationship and his faith, and reinforces the Jewish belief that we can seek God's help through prayer. But true to Jewish tradition, the young man does not simply wait for God's answer. Instead, he finds his own ingenious way out of a potentially tragic situation by being humorously clever in his "prayer" to God.

Once there was a Moroccan king who loved justice. He always wanted to know more about his people. He wanted to hear what they were thinking and learn what would make their lives better. He wanted to make sure that there was justice in the land. The king knew that he could not find the answers dressed in his royal robes. His people would never tell him the truth. They would only tell him what they thought he wanted to hear. So the king dressed himself in a disguise and joined crowds to hear what the people were really saying. Sometimes he even asked people questions and listened carefully to their answers.

One day the king disguised himself as a poor beggar and went for a walk around the town. He came to a small cottage where he heard the sounds of an oud and a man's voice singing a joyous song. When the king knocked, the music suddenly stopped and a young man named David opened the door. "Is a guest welcome in this house?" asked the king.

Seeing a poor, weary beggar, but not knowing that this was really the king, David invited him in for dinner. David recited the blessing over the bread and they began to eat.

After dinner, David began to play his oud and sing again. The king asked him about his life and how he earned his living.

40

"I am a cobbler. During the day I repair people's shoes. When I earn enough for my food, I go to the marketplace, buy what I need, and return home," replied David.

"And what about tomorrow? Do you not worry whether you will have enough for tomorrow?" asked the king.

"I have faith that all will be well tomorrow. Blessed be God, day by day," answered David.

As they bid each other a good night, the king said, "May I come again?"

David replied, "A good guest is always welcome."

When the king returned to his palace, he thought, "I will test this man's faith." He sent out a proclamation that no one was to hire cobblers who did not have a special permit.

The next morning, David realized that he could not earn any money from fixing shoes. Instead he decided to draw water from the well for people. Doing this, he earned enough money for his food.

When the king returned to David's cottage that night, again in disguise, he was very surprised to find that David had a table filled with food. After eating, David once again began playing his oud and singing. The king listened for a while and then asked David about the day.

David said, "Today I was not allowed to work as a cobbler because I did not have the special permit that the king demanded of cobblers. Instead I drew water from the well and sold it."

"And what will happen if the king forbids anyone from drawing water for others?" asked the king.

"Blessed be God, day by day," answered David.

The next day, the king gave an order that no one was to buy water from anyone who drew it from the wells. They must only draw water for themselves.

Once again David found that he needed to find a different kind of work. He decided to become a woodchopper and sold his wood to people.

That night the king again arrived at David's home and to his surprise found David about to sit down to his usual feast. When he asked how David found work that day, David replied that he had worked as a woodchopper.

"What if the king forbids anyone from chopping wood for others? Then what will you do?" asked the king.

"Blessed be God, day by day," replied David, and continued his singing.

The next day, the king ordered that all woodchoppers report to the palace to serve as palace guards. David came to the palace and was given a uniform and a sword and told to stand guard.

That evening when David went to collect his payment for the day's work, he was told that a special order had been given by the king that all guards would be paid only at the end of a week's time. What was he to do now? How would he buy food for his dinner?

Suddenly David had an idea. He decided to pledge the metal blade of his sword in exchange for food. When he received his wages at the end of the week, he could pay back the money and reclaim his sword. In that way, no one would know what he had done.

As soon as David returned home, he carved a wooden blade and connected it to the handle of his sword. Then he placed it in his scabbard so that it looked like a regular sword. "This way no one will suspect that it is not a real sword made of steel," he said to himself with a laugh.

As David was about to sit down to dinner, he heard a knock on the door. There was the same poor man, the king in disguise. Once again, David welcomed him in and invited the man to eat with him. The king was very surprised to see the delicious foods on the table, but he waited until after dinner to ask how David earned money that day.

David told his guest that he had become part of the king's guard. "But since I will not receive any pay until the end of the week, I pledged the steel blade of my sword and carved a wooden blade in its place," revealed David.

The king laughed at this clever deception and asked, "And what will you do if there's a sword inspection tomorrow?"

"Blessed be God, day by day," answered David.

With that, the king bid David a good night.

Now the king decided to test David's cleverness and he called David to him as he sat on the throne. The king knew David, but David could not recognize the king, for he had always come in disguise.

"Here is a man who has been found guilty of a terrible crime and sentenced to death. I have chosen you as the guard who must carry out the punishment with your sword. It must be done in front of the whole court," the king commanded.

"Please, Your Majesty, I have never killed anyone in my life. I cannot do this terrible deed," cried David.

"It is the king's order. Carry out the order," shouted the commander.

David began to tremble and pray. He didn't know what to do, but he knew that he had to do something—and quickly, too.

Suddenly he grabbed hold of the sword's handle in its sheath and spoke in a soft, quivering voice, as though someone else was speaking. He said, "Creator of the Universe, you know that I have never shed another man's blood. You know that I have never even used a sword. I do not want to kill anyone, but as this is the king's order, I will make an agreement with you. If this man is really guilty, then let my blade be made of steel. However, Creator of the Universe, if this man is really innocent, then turn my steel blade to wood."

All the people gathered there held their breath as David very slowly drew his sword from its sheath. The crowd gasped in amazement when they saw that the sword was made of wood.

The king ordered the immediate release of the prisoner.

Then, with a hearty laugh, he stood up from his throne, approached David, and embraced him. The king said, "I see now that your faith is truly strong and how it helps you through difficult times." He then revealed that he had been David's dinner guest night after night. The king appointed David as his wise advisor, and they remained honest friends from that day on.

David continued to say, "Blessed be God, day by day."

An Esrog as Big as a Horse

In Judaism, the esrog represents many things: a full heart, a bountiful harvest, and the fruit of Paradise, as the poor tailor Yehiel points out in this tale. It is with his whole heart that Yehiel sacrifices what he most desires— an esrog for Sukkos—reminding us that the highest Jewish value is giving of ourselves or our possessions to help another in greater need.

Once there was a poor man named Yehiel. Yehiel had the same wish every year. He wanted to buy the most beautiful, fragrant esrog he could for the festival of Sukkos. But perfect esrogrim were expensive because they had to be sent from the land of Israel, and each year he was only able to save enough for a very small, almost shriveled, green-tinged esrog. Even so, Yehiel celebrated each year with great joy in his heart as he waved his *lulav* and esrog and marched in the processions around the synagogue. Every year he promised himself that he would work harder and save even more money. "That way I will be able to buy the largest and most exquisite esrog," he said to himself.

Yehiel did not want the largest esrog to show off, heaven forbid, and certainly not to compete with the richest families in the town. No, those were not his intentions.

"Why do you want to have such an expensive esrog, my husband?" asked his wife, Malka.

"Because the esrog is the 'apple of Paradise,'" replied Yehiel. "I have heard that perhaps this was the very fruit that grew on the Tree of Knowledge in the Garden of Eden."

"Where did you hear this? Were you there?" asked Malka, laughing.

"Don't laugh, Malka. You know that I am not a learned man and cannot study the Torah or the Talmud myself, but I remember everything the rabbi says.

46

I remember how the rabbi talked about the woman in the Garden of Eden and how she wished to eat the fruit of that tree. The rabbi used the Hebrew word *ragag* for 'desire,' but I thought he said 'esrog.' When I asked, the rabbi told me that I was right—that the word esrog sounds like ragag. And that's why the rabbis believe that the esrog may have been the forbidden fruit in the Garden." Yehiel loved puns, wordplay, and wit.

"And besides," he continued, talking as though teaching his wife, "do you know that the esrog represents the heart? I always feel such joy in my heart when I hold the esrog and when I smell its lemony fragrance. But if I had a really extraordinary esrog, that would give me even greater pleasure during the seven days of the holiday."

All year long, Yehiel worked hard as a tailor. He even worked evenings to make extra money. "This year I will finally realize my dream of owning the finest esrog in the town," he said in his singsong way.

Just after Yom Kippur was over, Yehiel ate a meal with his family to break the fast and then started to build his *sukkah*. The next morning he set out for the marketplace to buy the best esrog there was.

On his way, he came upon a poor *balagole*—a horse-and-carriage driver. Yehiel saw that he was very upset.

"What's happened?" Yehiel asked him.

"Oy, a terrible calamity has befallen me. For so many years I had one horse that pulled my carriage. But just this morning my horse fell into a hole and, woe is me, I don't have any way to make a living anymore. Now I have no possible way to work and earn money," complained the driver.

Without a hesitation, Yehiel took out his whole savings and gave it to the man.

"Go and buy for yourself a horse that can pull your wagon so that you can earn a living," said Yehiel.

The poor driver blessed Yehiel and continued on his way to the marketplace to buy a horse. Meanwhile, Yehiel turned around to go back home.

When he arrived home, his wife looked to see what kind of esrog he had purchased but saw that his hands were empty.

"Where is the esrog you went to buy? What happened?" she asked with great curiosity and concern.

"Well, in truth, I bought an esrog as big as a horse," laughed Yehiel. Then he told Malka about meeting the poor driver whose horse had become crippled and could no longer pull his wagon. "I gave him all my savings so that he could buy another horse," concluded Yehiel. "This year I'll borrow someone else's esrog so that I can recite the blessings. And then maybe next year…"

News of Yehiel's good deed spread very quickly throughout the town. By the next morning, everyone had contributed some money and brought it to Yehiel. Yehiel took the money to the marketplace and carefully chose the largest and most beautiful esrog he had ever seen. He put the esrog into a special box to hold it in place so that the *pittam* would not break off.

When the holiday of Sukkos began two days later, Yehiel held the esrog upside down in his left hand with the pittam pointing down. He held the lulav—with its palm, myrtle, and willow leaves—in his right hand. Holding his two hands together, he recited the blessings. After carefully turning the esrog around so that the pittam pointed up, he began shaking the four species in six directions to show that God is everywhere. Then he inhaled deeply the heavenly citron fragrance of the esrog.

"Ah! This really smells of the Garden of Eden!" And his thankful heart danced happily as he passed the lulav and esrog around to the rest of the family.

Learning Wisdom by Observation

As this tale reminds us, it is better to be free than to be caged, no matter how kind our master is to us. The Jewish people have learned this lesson many times, as when they struggled for freedom from slavery in Egypt. At times, the speaking of certain words or the studying of the Torah was forbidden, forcing Jews to communicate in code, just as the characters in this story do.

Once there was a princess who had a beautiful bird in a cage. She had seen the bird while walking in her garden one day and called out to her handmaiden, "That bird! It's the most beautiful bird I have ever seen. I would like to have it where I can see it any time I like and hear it sing its sweet melody for me all day long."

Immediately the handmaiden ran to tell the servant of the princess's wish. The servant quickly got a long-handled net. He scooped up the innocent bird and put him into a golden cage. The princess kept the cage near her bed and took very good care of the bird. She lavished great attention on him and even fed him milk and honey. Her servant carried the cage wherever the princess walked in the palace or in the garden.

But no matter how loved he was, the bird was sad and did not want to remain in a cage. He wanted to fly freely into the trees, to sing with his bird friends, and to wing his way up in the sky.

One day the bird overheard the prince say that he was going to travel to another palace and would return in a month's time. The bird whistled and the prince turned toward his cage.

Then the bird said, "O Prince, when you go to this foreign land, would you do me a favor?"

The prince was surprised by the sound of the bird's voice, but replied, "Yes, I will gladly do you a favor. Would you like something special to eat?"

"No, I don't need anything special to eat. But should you happen to see any birds that look like me, will you tell them that one of their family is in a cage in the palace and sends his best regards? Will you do that for me?"

The prince agreed and left on his journey.

A month later, the prince returned and passed the bird's cage. The bird whistled and the prince turned to him.

"Did you see any of my family when you were on your travels?" the bird asked.

"Ah, yes, little bird. I did see a bird that looked like you," replied the prince.

"And did you send my regards as I asked you to do?" asked the bird.

"Yes, I did. I told the bird that you were in a cage in the palace and that you sent your best regards, as you requested," answered the prince.

"And what did my cousin reply?" asked the bird.

"Oh, dear bird, I am sorry to tell you that your cousin didn't say anything. You see, when I sent him your regards, he was sitting on a high tree branch. As soon as I gave him your message, he fell out of the tree and died," said the prince sadly. "When I went over to pick him up so that I could bury him properly, he flew away. So I do not have any message from your cousin after all."

The bird didn't say anything else to the prince.

The next morning, the handmaiden opened the drapes and window in the princess's bedroom. The princess stretched and turned to say good morning to her pet bird, as she always did. But she didn't hear any singing from the birdcage in response to her greeting. The princess jumped out of bed and took a closer look. What she saw made her cry out, "Oh, my bird is dead! Come quickly and help me."

Immediately the servant and the handmaiden came running over to where the princess was weeping and shouting. "Get up, my bird!" she was pleading. "Begin singing, please!"

But, alas, the bird was lying still at the bottom of the cage. Seeing that the bird was dead, the princess commanded, "Take the bird out of there. Toss it away."

The servant opened the cage door, carefully picked up the bird, and tossed it out of the open window. As soon as the bird felt the fresh air, he spread his wings and flew to the highest branch of the nearest tree.

The princess was as startled as the handmaiden and the servant.

"What is the meaning of this? Why did you leave my comfortable cage? Didn't I treat you well? How did you learn to trick me like this?" asked the princess.

The bird whistled and said, "Princess, the best cage in the world would not be as good as having the freedom to fly where I want. And since you asked how I learned to trick you into giving me my freedom, well, I learned it from my cousin who lives in a faraway land."

Then the bird whistled again. He flew in a spiral ever higher and was never again seen in the palace gardens.

The wise Daughter who solves riddles

This folktale, which focuses on riddles, is one of the most beloved in Jewish oral tradition. Jews have always loved riddle stories, such as the many popular legends of King Solomon. By understanding riddles and answering with wisdom and cleverness, the young woman in this story reminds us to appreciate what is most important in our lives.

One day two neighbors were walking to the city. On the way there, they saw three silver *dinars* and began to argue. One of them said, "I saw these dinars first."

"Not true," the other one said. "I saw the coins first."

Standing firm, the first one said, "Because you are my friend, I'll tell you what we should do. I'll take two of the dinars and *you* can have one."

The second one stubbornly replied, "No, because you are my friend, I'll take two and *you* can have one."

Finally they put the three coins into a leather sack. Both men held onto the bag until they reached the king's palace.

The friends came before the king and told him their story about finding the three coins. "I saw them first, so I should keep the dinars," insisted the first friend.

"That is not true. I saw them first and I deserve to have the dinars," argued the second friend.

"In order to decide who deserves these coins, I'll tell you a riddle," the king said. "The one who gives the right answer will get all three dinars. Here is the riddle: What is the fastest thing in the world?"

The first one replied, "There is nothing faster than the wind."

The king waited for an answer from the second friend, but he didn't have one. "O King, give me two days to think about the riddle," he asked.

The king agreed to this request, and the second friend returned to his house very worried. When his beloved daughter saw him, she asked, "What is wrong, Father? Why are you so sad?"

At first he didn't answer, but his daughter pleaded with him to tell her why he was so disturbed. Finally the man told his daughter everything that had happened to him since he and his friend had found the dinars.

The girl laughed and said, "Father, tell the king that there is nothing faster than the imagination."

On the second day, the man went to the king and gave his answer to the riddle. The king was surprised and said, "Tell me, who gave you this answer?"

The poor man was terrified and said, "My most precious daughter answered your question."

Then the king said, "Because of this answer, you deserve to win the dinars. But first, bring your daughter to me in three days' time. Tell her that she must come even if she is famished, even if she has no beautiful clothes, and even if she has no mount."

The father returned to his daughter and told her that the king wished to meet her "even if she is famished, even if she has no beautiful clothes, and even if she has no mount."

The girl laughed and said, "Father, I will go with you." On the third day, the girl ate only a handful of pumpkin seeds. Then she draped a cloth of delicate silk around her and rode to the king's court on a sheep.

The king was surprised at the girl's wisdom and said, "You are indeed wise to understand the meaning of my message. You are the woman destined to be my wife. You will be my queen, but only on the condition that you never interfere with the rule of my kingdom or with any of my judgments."

The young woman agreed and they were married.

Soon after that, two different friends came to the king. They had been having a dispute over two riddles. The two men could not agree on an answer, so they asked the king to solve the riddles for them.

"We know that you are fond of riddles, O King. Perhaps you can help us solve these riddles and settle the argument that we have been having for years," said one of the two men.

"Very well," replied the king. "I will hear the riddles."

"The first riddle is, 'What is the hardest thing in the world?'" said the first man.

"And the second riddle is, 'What is the sweetest thing in the world?'" said the second man.

The king thought awhile and said, "Of course, the hardest thing in the world is making a living and the sweetest thing in the world is honey." Then the king dismissed the friends.

But the two men were not satisfied with the king's answer and left his court feeling very disappointed.

The queen saw them leave and realized that they were not content with the king's judgment. She called the men to her and asked what the problem was. They told the queen what had happened in the king's court.

"The riddles are simple," the queen said. "Whether you are rich or poor, the hardest thing is to lose your memory. As for the sweetest thing, it is water. Someone who is thirsty will not drink honey."

The men went back to the king and told him their new answers. The king immediately knew that the queen had given them those answers. He quickly became angry that she had shamed him by giving wiser answers than his own.

The king went to the queen and commanded her to leave his palace. "Take with you the one thing that you most desire," he said. "Now go!"

"Your Majesty," the queen said to the king, "join me for one more dinner together before my departure. Just as we began our marriage with a feast, let us end our marriage with a feast."

The king agreed to this invitation, and the queen prepared a special dinner. When they were seated at the table, the king asked, "Have you decided what one thing you will take with you?"

The queen smiled at the king and said, "I looked throughout the whole palace, my dear king, but I couldn't find anything that I wish to take with me more than you."

The king gave a joyful laugh and replied, "If that is so, then you will remain as my queen. But I will serve you, my dear queen, for indeed I see that you are the wisest one after all."

Remember

Whether or not we want to remember, our past affects who we are. This story highlights the Jewish belief that we all have a responsibility to know and remember our past if we are to act properly in the present and plan for the future.

Long ago, in a faraway kingdom, a king died. In order to choose the new king, a strange ritual took place. The royal advisors released a bird known as the Bird of Happiness. Everyone watched carefully as the bird flew around and around a group of men. Whoever's head the bird finally settled down on was chosen as the new king.

It so happened that the bird came to rest on the head of a jester. Suddenly the jester found himself being lifted onto the shoulders of the king's advisors as everyone shouted, "Long live the new king!"

The jester was carried to the palace, where he was bathed in perfumed waters and given royal robes and a crown to wear in place of his old clothes—his ragged hat with bells and his jester's drum. But the new king insisted that he keep his old clothes and hat and drum.

The king's first order was that a small hut be built near the royal palace. When the hut was completed, the king went inside holding his old clothes and drum. He stayed only a few moments. When he left the hut, he had nothing in his hands. Then the king locked the door of the hut with a special key and went back to the palace.

The advisors were puzzled by this behavior, but they did not say anything to the king. What they did tell the new king was "Remember, you are now our king and you must act like a king at all times, not as a jester."

As the years went by, the advisors became more and more curious about the hut. Every once in a while, the king would enter the hut, stay a few moments, and then leave, always locking the door securely behind him. Finally one day when they saw him leaving, they asked the king why he went into the hut.

The king replied, "I remember your good advice to always act like a king. But I was a jester before I became a king. I keep my old clothes and drum in the hut. When I see them, I remember who I was and the people I came from. I remember how drumming my songs helped to make people happy and laugh. Remembering that reminds me to be a more compassionate, caring king."

And with that, the king returned to the palace.

A Detour Through Helm

The Talmud records many debates, including the one about the sun and the moon retold here. This debate leads to an important argument in Helm, a town where the inhabitants see the world in their own unique way. In this tale, the Helmites' own "wise" sense of logic helps them resolve a most important question.

Helm is known as the town of foolish people. Or maybe the people in Helm are really wise, after all. But Helm came into existence in a most interesting way.

You see, God sent out two angels, each with a sack of souls. One angel's sack was filled with handsome and intelligent souls. The other angel carried a sack filled with foolish souls. God instructed the angels to distribute the wise souls and the foolish souls equally wherever they flew.

One day, the angel carrying the foolish souls flew a little too low—or maybe the mountain peak was too high. The sack caught on the mountain peak, ripped open, and the foolish souls floated down into the valley. When the souls were born, they found that they liked it there. So they stayed in the valley and called the place Helm. And they were called Helmites.

One day, a great debate started in Helm. The Helmites were reading the Talmudic story about how God had created the two great lights in the sky—the sun and the moon. In the beginning, both of these lights were of equal size and equal brightness, each one throwing off fireballs.

The moon grumbled about this and complained to God that it needed more space to turn in the heavens. The moon proposed that the sun become a bit smaller so that the moon would have more room. "The fireballs from the sun keep hitting me. Just look at my pits and craters," said the moon.

But when God asked the sun if it was happy with the way it had been created, the sun said that it was satisfied. To settle the debate, God made the moon smaller and put it on the other side of the world to turn in the roomy nighttime sky by itself.

After they read this, the Helmites began debating which was more important, the sun or the moon.

"Which one is more important? What a question! The sun, of course," said one Helmite.

Another Helmite heard this remark and jumped in. "The sun? The sun? How can you be so foolish? The moon is more important! We need the moon more than the sun!"

Soon a crowd of Helmites had gathered in the marketplace. Each one took a side, either with the sun group or the moon group. They stayed there all day, forgetting even about going to work, and discussed and debated and argued and agonized. Everyone had an opinion, but no one would give in.

Since no one wanted to leave until his side had won, the Helmites all agreed not to go home for dinner. Instead, dinner would be eaten in the marketplace so that they could continue their debate. Soon, large pots appeared. The women served the men bowls of golden chicken soup. In the middle of each bowl were matzoh balls and little golden egg yolks known as *ayerlekh*. The sounds of so many Helmites eating—or rather slurping—chicken soup at one time sounded like an orchestra tuning up off-key.

Suddenly one voice shouted, "Helmites, look! These golden ayerlekh look just like the sun!"

"What are you talking about, you fool! They look like the moon!" another said.

Everyone had an opinion about what the golden egg yolks looked like. Some said like the sun. Some said like the moon. Soon they were debating with a renewed vigor and waving their soup spoons in the air. The chicken soup grew cold, was spilled, and was then forgotten. The Helmites never finished eating their dinner that night.

Months went by. Then it was the holiday of Simkhas Torah, a time when the reading of the Torah ends with the death of Moses and begins all over again with the creation of the world. The Helmites gathered in the synagogue to hear the reading and to talk about the beauty of the holiday.

"*Ay ay ay*, this is such a beautiful yom tov. Ending the Torah with the death of Moses and then beginning right away with the creation of the world—it's a circle round like the moon," said one Helmite.

"You mean like the sun," countered another Helmite.

That's all it took. One mention of the heavenly lights and everyone was taking sides and shouting, "Sun!" "Moon!" "Sun!" "No, moon!" and on and on and on.

Finally the rabbi called everyone to order to begin the reading from the Torah scroll. The Helmites took their seats and became quiet. Everything went well, and everyone listened and followed the reading in their books.

The rabbi started to read the opening verses of the Torah: "In the beginning God created the heaven and the earth."

Then he continued reading what God had created on each of the seven days. But when the rabbi recounted what happened on the fourth day, he read: "And God created the sun, the moon, and the stars." As soon as the rabbi mentioned

the sun and the moon, the debate immediately started all over again. No one even heard about the stars or any of the other great things that were created after that. Such a tumult!

Finally, the wise elders among the Helmites agreed that the debate had to end. They realized that the only way to settle the debate once and for all would be for everyone to vote on which was more important, the sun or the moon.

The day after the holiday, the Helmites took a vote. They counted the votes carefully, over and over. You see, everyone had to take a turn counting the votes.

Finally they were ready to announce the results. The Helmites overwhelmingly voted that the moon was more important. And why? Because in the daytime when there's light, there is no great need for the sun. But at night when it's dark, that's when you need the moon.

Now, if you understand their logic, then maybe, just maybe, you, too, are a Helmite.

The Boy Who Prayed with the Alphabet

The idea of an innocent or unlearned boy praying to God in his own words is especially popular in Jewish folktales. This story about one such boy reminds us of the Hasidic belief that praying from the heart is more acceptable to God than simply reciting a memorized prayer.

Once there was a poor, ignorant boy who took care of the sheep. The only thing he had ever learned was the *aleph-bet*. All day long he would sing the letters of the Hebrew alphabet. The sheep enjoyed hearing their shepherd's song, for he had a sweet voice.

Sometimes the boy and his father would go to the synagogue on Shabbat. They would sit in the back where the unlearned men sat. The young boy could not read the prayers. He could not sing the songs. He sat there listening and feeling happy just to know that he was part of the Jewish people. That much his father had taught him, for the father himself did not know many of the prayers.

The boy's mother had taught her son to recite the *aleph-bet*. She had learned the alphabet from her own mother. The boy loved to repeat the letters over and over. He loved the sound of each one.

One Shabbat, the boy went to the synagogue with his father. He listened to the cantor chant the beautiful prayers to God. He listened to the rabbi speak such wonderful-sounding words. He looked around at all the men in their prayer shawls praying and speaking directly to God. This boy, too, wanted to express his feelings of love for God.

Suddenly the young boy began to recite the *aleph-bet*. At first he spoke softly, but then his voice became louder and louder.

His father stopped him. "Be quiet!" he commanded in a loud whisper. "You don't know how to read the prayers. Stop talking nonsense. Show respect! You're in the synagogue."

The boy sat quietly, but after a while he began again.

Again the father stopped him. This time he put a hand on the boy's mouth and said, "The rabbi will hear you and throw us out for what you are doing. Sit without making a sound or I'll take you home."

So the boy sat quietly. But how long could he sit there when all around him he saw and felt the holiness of the day?

All of a sudden, the boy started to recite the alphabet again, even louder than before. Then, faster than his father could catch him, he jumped up from his seat and ran to the *bimah*.

"*Rebono shel Olam*, Ruler of the Universe, I know I am only a child. I want so much to sing the beautiful prayers to you, but I don't know them. All I know is the *aleph-bet*. Please, dear God, take these letters of the alphabet and rearrange them to form the words that mean what I want to say to you and what is in my heart."

When the father, the rabbi, and the congregation heard the boy's words, tears formed in their eyes. Then they all joined him in reciting, "*aleph, bet, daled, gimmel, hey, vav . . .*"

A Trickster Teaches a Lesson

Trickster characters in folktales have clever and creative ways to teach lessons. In this humorous story, Hershele the trickster carries logic beyond logic to teach us how to give with a more generous heart.

Hershele of Ostropol was a trickster. Like all tricksters, he was always poor and hungry, always looking for a free meal or a "loan" of some money. Whenever a stingy, greedy miser insulted him or refused to offer him a meal or a loan, Hershele was always more than ready to teach the man some manners or a lesson in generosity. Of course, Hershele never used violence. Oh no! That was not the trickster's way. Instead he used words and clever plans as his weapons. And his lessons always reached their mark.

One day a shopkeeper named Yankel closed the door on Hershele's plea for some money to buy a good meal for an upcoming holiday. Hershele walked around town the whole day before he found the perfect scheme to teach Yankel a lesson.

That evening Hershele knocked on Yankel's door. When Yankel answered and saw that it was Hershele, he said, "What! You again!" and began to shut the door. But Hershele put his foot in the door and said in a loud voice, "No, don't worry. I didn't come for any money. I just want to borrow a silver serving spoon from you—just to use during Shabbos. I promise I will give it back to you right after the Sabbath. I give you my word."

Now Yankel knew that an oath is sacred, so he said with some reluctance, "Very well. But it's just a loan and only for two days. Remember, bring the spoon back as soon as Shabbos is over!"

Then Yankel called to his servant to bring him a silver serving spoon, which he handed to Hershele.

Early the next morning, Hershele went to the silversmith and asked him to make him a small replica of the silver spoon. Now the silversmith was not so willing to do this without payment. He knew Hershele's reputation. But Hershele made a promise to bring him the money in three weeks.

As soon as Shabbos ended, Hershele went to Yankel's house. When Yankel opened the door, Hershele handed him the serving spoon and the small replica.

"What's this? I only loaned you the large serving spoon, Hershele," said Yankel.

"That's true, Yankel. But I came to wish you mazel tov. Your spoon gave birth, and being the honest person I am, I brought you both your spoon and the baby spoon," replied Hershele.

Yankel was delighted with the new addition to his silverware collection.

A few days went by, and Hershele returned to Yankel's house. Yankel was a little happier to see him and asked, "What can I do for you this time, Hershele?"

"Yankel, do you think you could loan me a candlestick for Shabbos?" asked Hershele.

Remembering what had happened with the spoon, Yankel ordered his servant to bring him an ornate candlestick. He gave it to Hershele, again with Hershele's promise to return it after the Sabbath.

Once again Hershele went to the silversmith and had a baby candlestick made.

After Shabbos, Hershele returned to Yankel's home. Yankel opened the door, and Hershele handed him the large candlestick along with the baby candlestick. "Congratulations, Yankel. Your candlestick gave birth last night," said Hershele.

The following Friday, Hershele again came to Yankel. This time Yankel greeted him with "*Sholom aleikhem*, Hershele! What can I loan you this time?"

"For this Shabbos I would like to drink from a beautiful *kiddush* cup," said Hershele.

"Of course! Of course! I have the most beautiful kiddush cup that there is. I had it especially designed just for me. One moment and I will get it myself," replied Yankel.

He returned a few moments later holding a magnificent gold kiddush cup, beautifully designed with precious rubies all around it. Yankel was only thinking how wonderful it would be to have a miniature cup like this one. As Hershele left, Yankel called out, "And remember to return the cup as soon as Shabbos ends."

When the Sabbath ended, Yankel waited with great anticipation and impatience for Hershele to bring him the gold kiddush cup and a baby cup. But Hershele did not appear that night. Hershele did not come the next day or the day after or the day after that, either.

Finally, a very angry Yankel went to Hershele's house. He stormed up to Hershele's door, knocked loudly, and called out his name. After a long time, Hershele opened his door just a crack.

"Yes? Who is there? What do you wish?" asked Hershele in a quiet, sad voice.

"It's me, Yankel! I want my gold kiddish cup returned. That's what I want!" said Yankel in a commanding tone.

"Oh, a terrible thing has happened, Yankel. I'm afraid to even tell you the bad news about the kiddush cup. But you must know what happened, so I'll tell you. I'm sorry to say that your kiddush cup has died," replied Hershele.

"What! That's impossible! How can a kiddush cup die?" demanded Yankel.

"If you can believe that a spoon and a candlestick can give birth, why can't you believe that a gold kiddush cup can die?" answered Hershele with a mischievous tone in his voice.

With that, Hershele closed the door and laughed heartily.

It is said that from that time on Yankel kept the tiny spoon and the tiny candlestick on a special shelf near the door. Whenever beggars came to Yankel's door for a meal or some money, he always looked at that special place and gave them a double donation with his full heart.

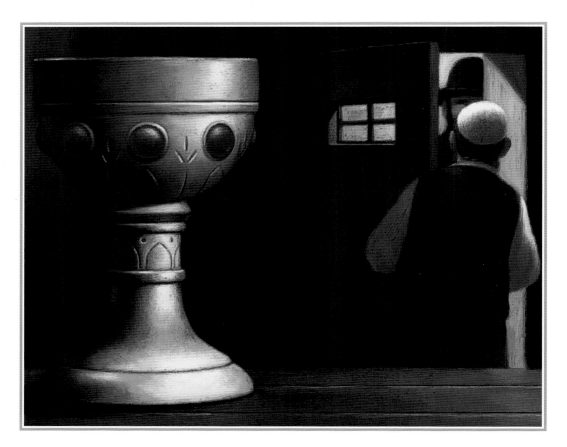

The Hungry Clothes

Tricksters are resourceful, clever, and shrewd, but they are also poor and always hungry. In this tale, Hershele uses his hunger to teach a well-deserved lesson in hospitality—a key theme in many Jewish folktales.

Hershele the trickster was often poor and hungry. He was always scheming to find a place at someone's table just as dinner was about to be served. Hershele himself looked like a big bear with a shaggy beard and ragged clothes. When people saw him approach—and they all knew who he was—they crossed the street. Who wanted to become engaged in conversation with Hershele, especially since he always managed to ask for money or a favor? Whenever he knocked on someone's door at dinnertime, someone inside the house would always ask, "Who's there?" When Hershele announced, "It's me, Hershele," the person would call out "Nobody's home. Come back tomorrow." So what could Hershele do but leave—and remain hungry.

Hershele knew that people stayed home on Shabbos to have a big dinner in honor of the special night. That's when Hershele knew he would eat well.

One Friday evening after his congregation had returned home from synagogue to welcome in the Shabbos, Hershele appeared at the home of one of the wealthiest families in Ostropol. As he walked toward the large house, Hershele could already smell the chicken soup, the roast chicken, the noodle and potato *kugels*, the carrot *tsimmes*, and the apple compote. His mouth began to water with the thought of feasting on such delicious foods.

Hershele got to the door just after all the guests had entered the house. Just as Meyer, the owner of the house, was about to close the door, he saw Hershele and said with a laugh, "Ah, Hershele. *Ay ay ay.* You should have come a little earlier. Did you dawdle after leaving the service? You came just a bit too late.

Besides, my table is full of dignitaries. I can't shame them by pushing you in between them. A good Shabbos to you." And Meyer closed the door, with Hershele still standing on the other side.

Hershele never took an insult lightly. Whenever someone insulted or rejected him, Hershele would say, "Whoever insults or rejects Hershele will soon learn a lesson."

He immediately left and began to think about how he would handle this rebuff. Suddenly he had an idea. He went to a friend's house and borrowed some of his finest clothing. When he was dressed in these well-tailored clothes, even Hershele looked like a nobleman. Hershele returned to Meyer's house and knocked on the door.

Meyer himself answered the knock. When he saw Hershele dressed up in such elegant clothes, he opened the door wider and said, "Hershele, we've been waiting for you. Come in. A good Shabbos to you!" Hershele was brought to the table, where he noticed that there was plenty of room and extra chairs.

The table was set with the finest china, silverware, and crystal goblets. The gefilte fish with horseradish and chicken soup with noodles had already been served. The servants put the dishes down in front of Hershele so that he could catch up with everyone, but Hershele waited to eat until all the food was placed on the table.

When the roast chicken, vegetables, and kugels were served, Hershele scooped up the foods and, one by one, started filling his pockets with them. The fish in his front vest pockets. The roast chicken and the potato kugel in his jacket pockets. More chicken and the noodle kugel were stuffed into his pants pockets. He put the vegetables into his inside pockets and stuffed the carrot tzimmes down his sleeves. Then he picked up the chicken soup with the noodles and poured some into each of his pockets. Each time he did this, he slurped and laughed a little louder.

Everyone at the table was aghast at the sight of Hershele feeding his clothes. Meyer just stared at him. His mouth was open as wide as the big round *hallah* on the table. Finally, he jumped up and started screaming, "Are you *meshuge*? You dressed up like a gentleman and tricked me into thinking you could sit and eat like a *mentsh*. A dressed-up ignoramus remains an ignoramus! What are you doing, you fool?"

But Hershele was not insulted because he knew that his actions had hit their mark. He was laughing as he finally said, "What am I doing, you ask? When I came to your house dressed in my torn beggar clothes, you didn't invite me to the Shabbos table. But as soon as I came back dressed like a gentleman, you invited me in as your guest. My clothes made all the difference. Since they were invited in, I'm feeding the dinner to my hungry clothes."

who is the laziest?

A tall tale is an improbable or greatly exaggerated story. Such entertaining and enlightening tales are common in Talmudic and rabbinic literature, as well as in the Sephardic and Ashkenazic cultures. In this "tall tale" contest of "Can you top this?" we realize that there is always someone who is indeed lazier.

Once there was a king who loved stories, contests, and entertainment. One day he came to court and found his jester asleep behind the throne.

The king was furious because he wanted to be entertained. He was in a terrible mood.

"Get up and entertain me!" the king shouted. "Dance! Sing! Play your flute! Tell me a joke that will make me laugh and cry at the same time! Tell me a story and keep telling it until you make me say stop. Why are you sleeping when the sun is shining? Surely you must be the laziest person in the world!"

Suddenly the king stopped screaming. "Aha! I have just had an idea. We'll have a contest to find the laziest person in the kingdom—someone even lazier than you, my dear jester. I will offer a great reward to this person."

On the day of the contest, hundreds of people came to the palace ready to recount their story of being so lazy that they would "out-lazy" everyone else. Each contestant was sure he would win the contest. The king sat on his throne ready to judge who the laziest person in his kingdom was. He couldn't wait to hear the stories and laugh at everyone's laziness. What could be better than that?

As each contestant approached the throne, the king asked, "And what story illustrates your laziness?"

One after another, the contestants offered their "lazy" stories. Some told their tales in a lively voice, some in a drone-like voice, some in a lazy drawl, and some sounded half-asleep. Although the king enjoyed their stories, he could not find the laziest person—yet. Finally there were three contestants left.

The first young man stepped up to tell his story. "Your Majesty, one day I was so hot and so parched with thirst that I sat down at the table to rest. Sweat was running down my face and I felt faint from the heat—that's how hot I was. I was so thirsty that my throat was as dry as sand on the hottest day in the desert. On the table was a huge glass of cool, fresh water. But I was so lazy that I felt I would rather die than lift up that glass to drink."

Then the second man told his story. "Your Majesty, I was sitting in my large rocking chair, but I was too lazy to rock. There on the table was my dinner

waiting for me. All my favorite foods were on the plate. Suddenly a cat jumped up on the table and began eating my dinner. I watched as the cat devoured my delicious dinner, because I was just too lazy to get up and shoo the cat away."

Finally the last young man stood before the king. The king asked him what story illustrated his laziness and then waited for a response. But the young man was too lazy even to answer.

The king waited and then announced, "The man who was too lazy to answer my question is surely the laziest person in the kingdom. He wins the contest."

HOW MUCH
IS a smell worth?

A story is a beautiful way to learn about the Jewish customs, foods, heroes, and rituals in the many lands where Jews have lived. This version of a popular folktale is set in the city of Marrakesh. Here, the community's judge is the Hakham, the chief rabbi in a community of Sephardic Jews. As with all the versions, this wise judge resolves this case in a clever way, matching sense to sense.

A long time ago, many of the Jews lived in the Mellah in Marrakesh under the protection of the Moroccan king. The Mellah was a walled community with a large arched entrance built near the king's palace. The Jews could go out freely to conduct their business, shop in the center of town or in the large marketplace, or visit with their friends and family who lived in the city. There were shops in the Mellah, too, but they did not have everything one might need. At night, the large gates of the Mellah were locked. Guards stood watch all night to protect the Jews inside.

In this Mellah there lived a poor young boy named Aaron. Aaron often left the Mellah after he had finished his day's studies. As he left, he would touch the green-painted wall of the arch and call out the name of Rabbi Mordechai Ben Atar. He didn't know why he did this, but his parents did it, so he did, too.

Then Aaron would walk down his favorite street in Marrakesh. Why was this his favorite street? Because it had the best bakery in the city. This shop had all of the delicious baked goods that Aaron loved so much. There were bakers in the Mellah, but they baked mostly *l'khebz de sheir* (black bread). That was all the poor Jews could afford to buy. Aaron loved to smell the round, sweet white bread and the baguettes at this bakery. He also loved the *kiks* (rectangular-shaped cookies), the *h'laouet* (little sweet pastries), and the *h'laouet coco* (coconut cookies).

79

Aaron would stop just near the doorway of the bakery and smell the fragrant air coming from the inside. Since he had only a few *dirham*, he could never buy anything. But he loved to say the names of the pastries in the Moroccan Judeo-Arabic language that they spoke at home. He felt like he was tasting the pastries as he spoke their names.

One day as Aaron was standing there inhaling the wonderful smells of the bakery, the baker came out and said in an angry voice, "I see you standing there smelling what I bake almost every day. You are stealing from me. You owe me money for this."

"But, sir, I don't have any money to pay you. Besides, I don't eat anything. I just stand and smell the pastries," replied Aaron.

But the baker was adamant that he should be paid for what the young boy was smelling.

Not knowing what to do, they went to the Hakham, a wise judge for the community. The Hakham was the rabbinical head of the Bet Din, the counsel to decide religious, business, legal, and personal matters. The baker presented his case first. Then the Hakham looked at the young boy and asked, "What do you say to this accusation?"

Aaron stood there frightened. He had never been to court before. He had always been honest, as he was taught. Now he would have to defend himself. Before he spoke, he prayed for Rabbi Mordechai Ben Atar to help him find the right words.

"It's true what the baker says. I stand outside of his shop and smell the baked cookies and breads. I wish I could pay him for some of those good things, but I have no money for any of them. So I satisfy myself with smelling them," replied Aaron.

"Do you have any money at all?" asked the Hakham.

"Well, I do have a few dirham in my pocket," answered Aaron.

Suddenly the Hakham gave a hearty laugh. "Good," he said. "Put the coins into this little velvet bag, hold it up, and shake it hard."

The poor young boy did as the Hakham instructed. His hands were shaking so hard from fright that the bag almost shook by itself. The coins jingled, sounding like muffled toy bells.

Then the Hakham said to the baker, "I judge that the sound of these coins is the just payment for the smell of your breads and pastries. One sense exchanged for another sense makes sense."

With his clever wit, the Hakham had settled the case wisely.

king solomon and the owl

This story emphasizes two of King Solomon's most prominent qualities: his ability to communicate with animals and his curiosity. Solomon legends often include dialogue with various animals, such as an eagle, which sometimes serves as his mode of transportation, an ant, from which he learns humility, and an ancient frog, who reveals what it considers to be the most peculiar thing it has ever seen. In this story, Solomon asks an owl a question and receives a wise, truth-filled answer.

King Solomon was known for his great wisdom. But how did he come to be so wise?

One night in a dream, God appeared to Solomon and said, "What do you wish for? Ask and I will grant it."

Solomon replied, "I wish for an understanding heart so that I may be wise in my judgments and truly listen to the people."

But Solomon was not only wise. He also loved questions and riddles. One day he called for the owl that made its nest close to the palace throne room.

"Dear owl, you are known for your wisdom in the bird kingdom, just as I am known for my wisdom in the human kingdom. I would like to know which is the prettiest bird in the whole bird kingdom."

The owl returned to its nest, scooped up something in its wings, and flew back to the palace. The owl came before King Solomon.

"King Solomon, here is my own baby owl. This is the prettiest bird in the whole world."

Then King Solomon had the answer to his question. For the mother, her child is the most beautiful of all creatures.

using your head in a tight situation

Many Jewish folktales center on the person whose cleverness prevails over the strength of a foe. In the tradition of David who slew the giant Goliath with a well-aimed stone from his slingshot, this humorous story of a quick-witted "hero" reminds us that one does not have to have power to get the upper hand.

A long time ago, a young man was riding his horse through the woods on his way back to the shop where he worked. Being a trustworthy apprentice, he had been sent to a neighboring town on business. Strapped to the side of his saddle was a large satchel filled with gold watches that he had purchased for his master. The horse was galloping at a rapid pace because the young man was nervous. It was not safe to be in the woods, especially with valuable merchandise. He was very anxious to get to the shop.

Suddenly another horse appeared from behind a tree and stopped in the middle of the apprentice's path. The young man drew in his reins. His horse slowed and stopped before they reached the horse blocking their path.

"Get off your horse or I'll shoot you off," said the man on the other horse.

"Very well," called out the frightened young man. "Just don't shoot. You see, I'm getting off my horse."

"Now slowly untie your satchel," said the forest robber. "But remember, I have my pistol aimed at you. I'll shoot if you make any sudden movements."

"Oh, I will do everything you tell me. I do not want to get shot. You see, I'm doing everything slowly just as you directed me to do," replied the young man with a trembling voice.

"Empty your pockets and put your watch and money in the satchel. Then bring the satchel to me."

Again the young man did everything the robber asked.

Then while he was closing the clasp of the satchel and giving it to the robber, the young man suddenly spoke again. "Mister, this satchel contains gold watches that I was sent to buy for my master's customers. When I return without them, he will accuse me of theft and I will be jailed. My good name will be spoiled. I must convince my master that I was really robbed of these watches. Will you help me?"

Impatiently the robber said, "Sure! Sure! What is it that you want me to do? Be quick about it. And remember, I have my pistol aimed at you. Don't try anything stupid."

"No! No! I won't do anything. I just want you to shoot into my clothes so that my master will know that I had no choice but to give up the watches. Here, I'll take off my hat and hold it up. You just have to shoot a few bullets into the hat. It will look like a narrow escape for me," said the young man.

"Sure, I can do that for you," replied the robber as he aimed and shot a few bullets into the young man's hat.

"That's good! Oh, but I will hold up my overcoat so that you can also shoot a few bullets into it. Then my master will be convinced that I met with a dangerous robber," said the young man, taking off his overcoat and holding it out for the robber to shoot at.

"Oh, shoot it one more time. Here, through the pocket," said the young man, throwing the coat into the air.

The robber aimed and shot, but all he heard was a click. He had no more bullets left in his pistol. The young man, counting each bullet, bravely ran over to the robber and pushed him hard. Knocking the pistol out of his hand, he grabbed the satchel filled with gold watches and then quickly jumped on his horse. He galloped away as fast as he could.

When he told the story to his master, his master laughed heartily and said, "Now that's using your head in a tight situation." Not only did the young man get a big reward and some new clothes, but he also had a story to tell to anyone who would listen.

the scratched diamond

When disaster strikes and something we treasure gets damaged, we have choices about our reactions. Sometimes we need to change the way we look at an imperfection and transform it into something positive and interesting. Changing perspective, or seeing things in a new way, is a very Jewish philosophy that we especially apply to Torah. It is written of the Torah in Ethics of the Fathers: "Turn it, and turn it, for everything is in it." In that way, we find at least seventy interpretations. So, too, we can apply this story of a scratched diamond to how we view life, in order to give us a happier perspective when things are not always perfect.

The Maggid of Dubno was known for his parables. Whenever someone asked him a question, he would always answer with a story.

One day a student was walking with the Maggid of Dubno and said, "Rabbi, I have many imperfections, many faults. How can I change them so that I can become a better person?"

The Maggid said, "Listen and I'll tell you a story.

"Once there was a king who owned one of the most splendid diamonds in the world. He was very proud of that flawless diamond and showed it off to all of his visiting dignitaries.

"One day the king noticed that the diamond had developed a flaw. There was a deep scratch in the precious jewel. He immediately called for the finest diamond cutters in the kingdom to come to the palace. 'You are artists in your work. What can you do to return the diamond to the way it was?' asked the king.

"But none of the diamond experts could promise that the diamond would ever be restored to its original perfection. Then a young man who had just completed his apprenticeship with the greatest of the diamond artisans said to the king, 'Your Majesty, while it is not possible to restore this diamond, as

the other diamond cutters have already told you, I would be willing to undertake the responsibility of creating a beautiful diamond out of this blemish.'

"The king had no other hope, so he gave his consent to the young man.

"The young man worked hard, but in secrecy. When he had finished his work, he presented the diamond to the king. When the king looked at it, he smiled with great satisfaction. Instead of seeing the scratch in the diamond as a blemish, the young diamond cutter had seen it as the stem of a rose. He had etched the roots, the flower, and the leaves onto the stem. In doing so, he transformed the scratch in the diamond into a mark of beauty. The diamond with its rose engraving became the most original and magnificent stone in the entire kingdom, and more precious to the king than before."

The Maggid turned to his student and said, "Just like the diamond with the scratch, we all have faults and blemishes. It's up to us to transform them into something of beauty and value."

Then the Maggid of Dubno and his student continued on their walk.

glossary

Aggadah—Sections of Talmud and Midrash containing sermon-like narratives from the Bible, stories, legends, folklore, anecdotes, and maxims: Aggada (lore) is found throughout the Talmud, and deals with the spirit, rather than the letter, of the law.

Aleph-bet—The first two letters of the Hebrew alphabet as well as the Hebrew word for alphabet.

Ashkenazim—Jews who lived in or whose ancestors came from Central and Eastern Europe and spoke Yiddish.

Ayerlekh—Unborn chicken eggs that are just yolks. (Yiddish)

Balagole—Horse-and-carriage driver.

BCE—Before the Common Era. Equivalent to BC.

Ben Atar, Rabbi Mordechai—A rabbi who lived at the turn of the eighteenth century and was known to perform miracles and give wise advice to those in trouble. It is said that his staff is embedded in the wall at the entrance of the Mellah in Marrakesh, Morocco. People touch the wall and call out his name when they need his help.

Bet Din—The rabbinical counsel who decided religious, legal, personal, and business cases. (Hebrew)

Bimah—The prayer stand or elevated platform on which the prayer stand is placed in the synagogue. (Hebrew)

CE—Common Era. Equivalent to AD.

Dinar—The basic monetary unit used in Iraq, Yemen, and other Arabic Middle East countries from the eighth century to the nineteenth century.

Dirham—The basic monetary unit used in Morocco.

Ethics of the Fathers—known as *Pirkei Avot* (Hebrew), one of the most popular works in Judaism. It is a classic Judaic text from the Mishnah containing religio-ethical wisdom. These timeless teachings are from the sages of the third century BCE to the third century CE.

Esrog—A citrus fruit that resembles a large but bump-filled lemon and over which a blessing is said on Sukkot. It may have been the original "apple of Paradise" that grew on the Tree of Knowledge. It is one of the four species of agricultural produce used on the harvest festival of Sukkot along with the *lulav* (made up of palm, myrtle, and willow branches).

Symbolically, the esrog has been compared to the heart of a person, the palm to the spine, the myrtle to the eyes, and the willow to the mouth. The Sephardic pronunciation of esrog is "etrog."

Gam zeh ya'avor—"This too shall pass." (Hebrew)

Hadrian—Hadrian (117–148 CE) was the Roman emperor and ruled over Judea 132–135 CE.

Hakham—The wise judge and rabbi of a Sephardic community. (Hebrew)

Hallah—A braided white bread baked special for the Sabbath. (Hebrew)

Hasidim—The Hasidim (literally, "the pious ones") are a Jewish religious sect, founded by Rabbi Israel the Baal Shem Tov (Master of the Good Name) in the eighteenth century. The emphasis was on faith and joy in prayer through song, story, and dance.

Hebrew—The sacred language of the Jewish people. The Torah and Talmud are written in Hebrew. It is the official language of the State of Israel.

Helm—The legendary setting for the Jewish "fool of the world" tales. The pronunciation of the "H" in Helm is like the final sound of "yuch."

Helmite—An inhabitant of the town of Helm. Someone who is foolish is often called a *Helmer hokhom* (a "Helm wise man"), but it is said sarcastically.

Israel Folktale Archives (IFA)—These extraordinary and important archives were founded by folklorist Dov Noy in 1955 in Israel. The archives, housed at Haifa University, contain more than 23,000 folktales collected from the various ethnic communities who live in Israel. The folktales are classified according to tale types and motifs.

Joshua—Rabbi Joshua, son of Hananya, was a great scholar and teacher who taught the Talmud orally during the first to second centuries CE. Such a teacher was known as a tanna ("repeater"), also referred to as a "living book," because the Talmud, or Oral Law, had not yet been written down.

Kiddush—"Sanctification." The prayer over wine recited at the beginning of Sabbath and holiday meals.

Kugel—A pudding of noodles or potatoes. (Yiddish)

Lulav—A bundle of branches and leaves from three trees: palm, willow, and myrtle. It is used along with the esrog during Sukkot to symbolize the fruit and trees, or the natural beauty, of Israel. When we recite the blessing over the four elements and shake them in the six directions in a circular shape, we acknowledge with our entire being that God is everywhere.

Maggid—A traveling rabbi who teaches about Judaism through stories. One of the most famous is the Maggid of Dubno (1741–1804) who was Rabbi Jacob Kranz. Called the "Jewish Aesop," he developed the parable especially for teaching the key values of Judaism.

Mazel Tov—"Good luck." (Hebrew)

Mellah—The protected walled-in area where Jews lived in Moroccan cities.

Mentsh—A compassionate, caring, and considerate human being. (Yiddish)

Meshuge—Crazy. (Yiddish)

Midrash (midrashim, plural)—Literally, "to seek out" or "to interpret." This is a type of rabbinic story that interprets and expands a biblical text in a story form. Midrashim were primarily written and collected during medieval times. The term refers to both the method of interpretation and the stories themselves. (Hebrew)

Mitzvot (mitzva, singular)—Commandments; good deeds. (Hebrew)

Oud—A musical instrument made from a pear-shaped gourd that has eleven strings. Popular in northern Africa and southwest Asia, it resembles a lute.

Parables—Brief tales that make a point quickly, usually through humor or a surprise ending. A parable is really a form of riddle, as it opens with a question and is then followed by a core story that supplies the answer in a coded form. The story ends with a lesson we can apply to our lives. There is an *aggadic* saying about parables: "With a tiny candle, one may still find a lost gold coin or a precious jewel." So, too, with a simple parable, one can learn a valuable lesson.

Pittam—The stem of the *esrog*. Without this stem, the esrog is not complete and cannot be used to perform rituals on Sukkot. (Hebrew)

Pomegranate—A fruit that resembles a larger but lumpy version of an apple and is often called a "Chinese apple." Its name comes from the Middle French for "seeded apple" (*pome garnete*). It is one of the choice fruits of Israel. Because of its many juicy kernels, it has become a symbol of fertility and plenty.

Ragag—Hebrew word that means "desire."

Rebono shel Olam—Literally, "Master of the Universe." (Hebrew)

Sephardim—Jews who were forced out of Spain in 1492. They settled in many countries, especially in the Middle East, Europe, Northern Africa, and America. The Arabic culture had a strong influence on many of the Sephardic folktales and folk songs. Their Jewish vernacular language is Ladino, Judeo-Spanish.

Shabbat—Sabbath in Hebrew.

Shabbos—Sabbath in Yiddish.

Shalom Aleikhem—A greeting meaning "Peace be unto you." (Hebrew)

Simkhas Torah—The holy day that immediately follows Sukkot. This is when the annual reading of the Torah is completed with the death of Moses and begins again with the creation of the world.

Solomon—Solomon was a king of Israel in the tenth century BCE. As one of the most popular heroes in Jewish folklore and legend, he is known for his great wisdom. Solomon was also said to speak the language of the animals.

Sukkot—Literally, "booths." Also known as the Festival of Tabernacles, Sukkot begins on the fifteenth day of the Hebrew month of Tishri, four days after Yom Kippur. It commemorates the booths in which the Israelites lived as they crossed the desert after the Exodus from Egypt. On this holiday, Jews build a temporary booth called a *sukkah* where they eat and sleep. Sukkot lasts for seven days and is immediately followed by another festival, Simkhas Torah. Sukkot is also a holiday celebrating the fall harvest. (The Yiddish/Ashkenazic pronunciation of Sukkot is "Sukkos.")

Talmud—The commentaries on the Torah; the Oral Law that was transmitted orally through the generations until the second and third centuries CE when it was codified and written down. It is the storehouse of Jewish history, law, stories, interpretations, debates, and customs, combining law and lore. The Torah and the Talmud are the two most sacred Jewish texts.

Torah—The first five books of Moses, or the Hebrew Bible; also known as the Pentateuch.

Tzimmes—A carrot stew (sometimes also made with meat and potatoes). (Yiddish)

Vizier—A high officer or adviser to the kings in Arabic countries.

Yiddish—The Jewish "everyday," or vernacular, language spoken primarily by the Jews of Eastern Europe. It is a mixture of medieval German, French, and Slavic languages combined with the sacred Hebrew language. Yiddish is written with the Hebrew alphabet.

Yom Tov—A holy day or holiday. (Hebrew)

sources

Honi the Circle Maker: This story is found in the Talmud Ta'anit 23a. In another Talmudic legend, Honi sleeps for seventy years. He has become known as the "Jewish Rip Van Winkle."

The Pots of Honey: Versions of this story can be found in Moses Gaster's two collections of Talmudic, midrashic, and folk tales—The Exempla of the Rabbis (1924: 1968) and The Ma'aseh Book (1934). It can also be found in Micha Joseph Bin Gorion's classic Mimekor Yisrael (1976). In other traditional versions of this folktale, it is either King David or King Solomon who decides who is telling the truth.

The Right Lessons: This story can be found in the Talmud Eruvin 53b, as well as in Moses Gaster's two books, The Exempla of the Rabbis and The Ma'aseh Book. The last part of the story when the rabbi asks the young girl about her basket actually comes from a different story found in Gaster's The Exempla of the Rabbis. It fit in so well with Rabbi Joshua's teachings about learning from younger people that I added it to this story.

The Figs: This popular story from the Jewish oral tradition can be found in the Talmud Yevamot, in Moses Gaster's The Exempla of the Rabbis, and in many midrashic collections, including Tanhuma and Midrash Hagadol. According to the Torah, we are not allowed to eat the fruit of a tree for the first three years after it has been planted (Leviticus 19:23).

The Pomegranate Seed: It is said that King Solomon designed his royal crown based on the crown of petals growing from the top of the pomegranate. This story about a single pomegranate seed can be found in Moses Gaster's collection of Talmudic and folk tales, The Exempla of the Rabbis, as well as in W. A. Clouston's Popular Tales and Fictions I (1887).

The Flour and the Wind: This popular legend appears in many sources, including Moses Gaster's The Exempla of the Rabbis, M. J. Bin Gorion's Mimekor Yisrael, Louis Ginzberg's The Legends of the Jews VI, and Hayyim Nahman Bialik's And It Came to Pass: Legends and Stories about King David and King Solomon. Two versions can also be found in the Israel Folktale Archives in Dov Noy's The Golden Feather (1976) from the Jewish-Greek oral tradition and in Noy's Jefet Schwili Tells: 195 Yemenite Folktales from Yemen (1963).

The Half Blanket: One of the best-known teaching tales in world folklore, this story exists in many versions and in many other cultures. This adaptation comes from Moses Gaster's The Exempla of the Rabbis. The Israel Folktale Archives also contain two versions: an Iraqi tale from Eliezer Marcus's Min Ha-Mabua (1966) and a story from Buczacz in Aliza Shenhar's book, Honor Your Mother (1969). In another version of this story, the grandfather is given a wooden bowl to eat from instead of a half blanket for warmth.

This Too Shall Pass: This story is interwoven into the midrashic narrative in Louis Ginzberg's The Legends of the Jews IV (1909–1938). It can also be found as "King Solomon's Ring" in Judith Ish-Kishor's Tales from the Wise Men of Israel (1962). Dov Noy includes a Turkish version from the Israel Folktale Archives in his Folktales of Israel (1963).

The Wooden Sword: There are a number of universal versions of this story that come from Turkey, Greece, Finland, Germany, Czechoslovakia, Italy, and Uzbekistan. It seems that when the listeners are "in on the joke," they love folktales with a surprise and clever happy ending. The Jewish versions of this tale, found in the Israel Folktale Archives, appear in Dov Noy's Folktales of Israel *(1963)* from Afghanistan, and a Sephardic Jewish text in A. D. L. Palacin's Cuentos Populares de los Judios del nort de Marruecos *(1952).*

An Esrog As Big As a Horse: No one is sure which fruit grew on the Tree of Knowledge. The fruit most often associated with this tree is the apple that Eve fed to Adam, but other fruits have been linked to the Garden of Eden as well, including the fig, the apricot, the pomegranate, and, as in this story, the esrog. A German version of this story can be found in the Israel Folktale Archives in Aliza Shenhar's A Tale for Each Month 1973 *(1974),* along with a Hasidic version from M. Beker's Parparot Le'Torah *(1981–1985).*

Learning Wisdom by Observation: One of the earliest Jewish sources for this story is in Berechiah Hanakdan's medieval text, Mishle Shualim (Fox Fables) *(1921; 1946).* Another example of a coded message communicating what could not be expressed securely in words appears in a Talmudic story, "Advice and Hints: A Tale of Antoninus and Rabbi Judah," found in M. J. Bin Gorion's Mimekor Yisrael. *In this story, the emperor Antoninus sends a messenger to Rabbi Yehuda Ha-Nasi for advice about how to save his dwindling royal treasury. The rabbi responds by digging up the large vegetables in his garden and replacing them with small vegetables, which the emperor understands to mean that his chief tax collectors must be replaced with honest officials.*

The Wise Daughter Who Solves Riddles: Many of the riddles posed in this folktale appear in other stories, both Jewish and universal, although they sometimes have different answers. This version of the story is a combination of two IFA stories, one from Iran and the other from Yemen. The last episode of the story, in which the wife chooses her husband, comes from a midrash in Pesikta. In all, the IFA contains more than eighty variations of this popular tale.

Remember: An IFA story from Iraq, this tale appears in Dov Noy's Folktales of Israel *(1963)* under the title "A Servant When He Reigns." It can also be found in Molly Cone's Who Knows Ten? *(1998),* as "The Reminder," and as "The Bird of Happiness" in Howard Schwartz's Jerusalem of Gold: Jewish Stories of the Enchanted City *(2004).*

A Detour through Helm: Almost every culture has a "fool of the world" story. In England they tell "The Wise Men of Gotham," in Germany they tell "The Wise Men of Schildburg," and so on. For Jews, the "fool of the world" stories take place in Helm, a legendary town in Poland. The terms wise men and fools are used interchangeably in these stories, because there is a constant debate over whether these people are wise or foolish. Tales about Helm can be found in many collections, including Solomon Simon's two volumes, The Wise Men of Helm *(1945)* and More Wise Men of Helm *(1965),* and Isaac Bashevis Singer's Zlateh the Goat *(1966).* The Talmudic tale of the sun and moon debate is from Talmud Hulin 60b.

The Boy Who Prayed with the Alphabet: This story can be found in several Hasidic collections, including Kehal Hasidim Hehadash, *a book published in Lemberg, Poland, in the early nineteenth century,* and in I. J. Y. Safrin's Emunat Tsaddikim *(1964).* In other versions of the story, the child plays a pipe or a whistle instead of reciting the letters of the alphabet. The story is identified closely with the Baal Shem Tov, the founder of Hasidism.

A Trickster Teaches a Lesson: Trickster tales are found in every culture. Some cultures, such as the Native Americans and the Jews, have more than one trickster. In the Sephardic oral tradition, the trickster is Joha, who is also the much-loved Arabic trickster. Hershele is the Ashkenazic trickster of Eastern Europe. This story about Hershele the trickster can be found in Dov Noy's Faithful Guardians (1976) and Edna Cheichel's A Tale for Each Month 1972 (1973).

The Hungry Clothes: This humorous story is one of the most popular teaching tales about hospitality in the Middle East as well as around the world. It has been told about trickster characters from every culture, including Anansi the Spider (African), Coyote (Native American), Nasr-ed-Din Hodja (Turkey), and Guifa (Italy). This version of the tale can be found in Dov Noy's A Tale for Each Month 1961 (1962).

Who Is the Laziest?: Tales with "Can you top this?" contests are very popular in world folklore. Sometimes there is a story-loving king who challenges the contestants to tell him stories without an end or to tell a story until he shouts "Enough!" It takes ingenuity, cleverness, and a different perspective to "win" the contest. This particular tall tale about being lazy can be found in the Israel Folktale Archives from Egypt.

How Much Is a Smell Worth?: One of the most popular universal folktales, this story is found in many cultures and in many versions. In Jewish folktales, King Solomon is usually the judge who decides how much the one who smells the food should pay the baker. There are twenty Jewish versions of this tale, including an Iraqi story from Dov Noy's Am Oved: Jewish-Iraqi Folktales (1965) and a Yemenite version from Dov Noy's Jefet Schwili Tells: 195 Yemenite Folktales (1963). There are also variants from Morocco ("The Cost of Meat") and another version from Iraq ("The Tale of a Cook and a Passerby").

King Solomon and the Owl: The first part of this story of how Solomon gains his wisdom comes from the First Book of Kings 3:5-13, and his ability to communicate with animals comes from midrash. This "owl" tale comes from the Israel Folktale Archives, specifically from Rumania in J. Avitsuk's The Tree That Absorbed Tears (1965), Dov Noy's Jewish Animal Tales (1973), and S. Falah and A. Shenhar's Druse Folktales (1978).

Using Your Head in a Tight Situation: This tale is a universal story found in Lithuanian, Flemish, Dutch, German, Russian, Korean, Spanish-American (U.S.), and Scottish folklore. It also appears in many versions in the Jewish oral tradition. A version called "The Jew and the Robber" can be found in Aliza Shenhar's A Tale for Each Month 1973 (1974). The idea of the pistol dates back to the eighteenth century and refers specifically to a small firearm.

The Scratched Diamond: The Maggid of Dubno lived in the 1700s and was especially beloved for his parables. Through his stories, he would teach Judaism and Jewish values. This particular story is adapted from "The Sound of the Shofar" in Benno Heinemann's The Maggid of Dubno and His Parables (1978). Two other versions, "The Blemish on the Diamond" from Nathan Ausubel's A Treasury of Jewish Folklore (1989) and "The Blemish on the Diamond" from Simon Certner's 101 Jewish Stories (1961), were both based on the parables of the Preacher of Dubno.